Grumb...

A little story
about having a happy attitude

V. GILBERT BEERS

ILLUSTRATIONS · BY · HELEN ENDRES

HARVEST HOUSE PUBLISHERS
Eugene, Oregon 97402

Library of Congress Cataloging-in-Publication Data

Beers, V. Gilbert (Victor Gilbert), 1928-
   Grumbleweeds: a muffin miniature.

   Summary: Mini discovers that her constant complaining while helping Poppi
and Mommi weed the garden has created an epidemic of grumbleweeds.
   [1. Gardening—Fiction.   2. Behavior—Fiction.   3. Conduct of life—
Fiction]   I. Title.
PZ7.B3875Gr 1988   [Fic]   88-80702
ISBN 0-89081-692-1

Copyright © 1988 by V. Gilbert Beers
Published by Harvest House Publishers
Eugene, Oregon 97402

Printed and bound in Singapore by Tien Wah Press (PTE) Ltd.

This Book Belongs To:

_____

_____

"In everything you do, stay away from complaining..."

Philippians 2:14 (TLB)

Mini Muffin did not want to pull weeds. She wanted to play. But Mommi said playing would be more fun when the chores were done. And Poppi said their backyard picnic would be more fun if they didn't have to look at weeds.

That's why they decided to pull weeds.

"Not fair," Mini complained. Then she began to grumble about anything and everything.

Under the forsythia bush Mini complained that it was too hard to crawl under bushes. "I'll get scratched under here," she grumbled.

Poppi said it was fun doing things together. Mommi said the yard would look nice when they were through.

But Mini grumbled anyway.

At the pansy bed
Mini grumbled about the
size of the pansies.
"Why don't these things
grow bigger so they will
choke out the weeds?"
she complained.

Poppi talked about
the fluffy clouds in the
sky. Mommi said they
should all be glad for the
fresh air and exercise.

But Mini grumbled
anyway.

When Mini reached the roses, she complained about the thorns. "These nice green weeds don't have thorns," she said. "Why don't we pull out the roses and leave the pretty green weeds?"

Poppi talked about how good the roses smelled. Mommi mentioned the bright colors.

But Mini grumbled anyway.

At the irises, Mini said there were too many weeds. "I'll be here all day," she said. "Maybe I'll be here all week. Who knows, I may just live here from now on."

Poppi talked about the fun they would have with a picnic lunch later. Mommi mentioned some of the good things they would have to eat.

But Mini grumbled anyway.

When Mini came to the peony plants, she grumbled about the heat. "The sun is killing me," she complained. "When I die of sunstroke someone will pick all these old flowers and put them on me. Then they'll be sorry I worked so hard."

Poppi almost laughed at that one. Mommi didn't think it was funny at all.

"Wonder what the next grumble will be?" Poppi whispered to Mommi. He didn't have to wait long, only as long as it took Mini to get to the geranium bed.

"My time is MUCH too valuable for these old weeds," she complained. "Think of all the con-STRUCK-tive things I could be doing."

Poppi chuckled. Mommi cleared her throat and frowned.

Poppi quietly left his weeding. He went to the forsythia bush where Mini had started. Then he walked to each place where Mini had pulled weeds. At each place he shook his head and said, "Hmmmm."

Mini stopped weeding. She watched Poppi. Each time he said "hmmmm" Mini became more curious.

At last Mini could stand it no longer. "Did I miss some weeds at each place?" Mini asked.

"It's not the weeds you missed that bother me," said Poppi. "It's the weeds you planted."

Mini looked puzzled. She didn't remember planting any weeds.

"What weeds?" Mini asked.

"Grumbleweeds!" said Poppi. "Each time you pulled green weeds you planted grumbleweeds. Look under the forsythia bush. Here are some I'LL GET SCRATCHED weeds. Do you see the WHY DON'T THOSE THINGS GET BIGGER weeds among the pansies? And those WHY DON'T WE PULL THEM OUT weeds with the roses. Do you see them?"

Mini almost thought
she did see the
grumbleweeds. They
really were quite ugly.
They were even uglier
than the green weeds.

"Stop! I don't want
to see any more
grumbleweeds," said
Mini.

"But what should we
do with them?" Poppi
asked. "We can't just
leave them there."

"I'm going to pull
them out!" said Mini.

Mini went to each
flower bed. She huffed

and puffed as she pulled
out each grumbleweed.
But she didn't grumble
once.

"There!" Mini said
at last. "No more green
weeds and no more
grumbleweeds."

"But lots of time for
play and a backyard
picnic," said Poppi.

Would you like to
have a picnic lunch with
The Muffin Family
today? If you do, you
will not see even one
green weed or one
grumbleweed.

Meet the Muffin Family and Their Friends